Bebe's Bad Dream

G. BRIAN KARAS

Greenwillow Books
An Imprint of HarperCollinsPublishers

Acrylic, gouache, and pencil were used for the full-color art.
The text type is Benguiat Gothic Bold BT.

Bebe's Bad Dream
Copyright © 2000 by G. Brian Karas
Printed in Singapore by Tien Wah Press. All rights reserved.
http://www.harperchildrens.com

Library of Congress Cataloging-in-Publication Data
Karas, G. Brian.
Bebe's bad dream / by G. Brian Karas.
p.   cm.
"Greenwillow Books."
Summary: Despite her mother's reassurances,
a young girl is convinced that aliens are coming to eat her,
until she decides to trick them into taking her brother instead.
ISBN 0-688-16182-0 (trade).   ISBN 0-688-16183-9 (lib. bdg.)
[1. Nightmares—Fiction.   2. Brothers and sisters—Fiction.
3. Extraterrestrials—Fiction.]   I. Title.
PZ7.K1296Be   2000
[E]—dc21   99-20087   CIP

1 2 3 4 5 6 7 8 9 10   First Edition

For my sister
and brother

When Bebe got ready for bed,
she put on her pajamas and her armor.

"Mom, Bebe's wearing armor to bed," said Bebe's
brother, Walter.

Bebe growled at Walter. "I know you dug up Mom's
garden looking for worms. Just wait until she finds out,"
she said.

"No armor, Bebe," called Bebe's mother from downstairs.
"It will rip the sheets."

Bebe's mother came in for good-night kisses.
"Ouch," she said as she sat on the bed—and Bebe's
helmet, shield, and laser.

"I need protection from the aliens," said Bebe.
"Oh, Bebe, not those awful aliens again. A bad dream,
 that's all they are."
"No, they're real. They want to eat me for dinner!"
 Walter made munching noises. "Yum. Bebe sandwiches."
"Walter, in your room!" said Bebe's mother.

Bebe's mother tucked Bebe in.

"I have proof they're not a dream," Bebe told her.
"I see them in the daytime, too." Bebe put on her
safety goggles.

"Bebe, no safety goggles in bed!" said her mother.

"Safety goggles won't rip my sheets," said Bebe.
"They protect my eyes from harmful rays."

"Okay, but only if you close your eyes. And no more
scary dreams. We are having sweet dreams tonight."

Bebe pretended to go to sleep. *Kuhhh-phewww, kuhhh-phewww,* she snored. But when her mother left, Bebe opened her eyes and checked around. Helmet, shield, and laser. It would take her only a second to reach them. Bedroom door, open just right. And Walter's room down the hall. It would be so perfect if the aliens took him and disappeared forever.

Bebe tried to stay awake by closing her eyes for two seconds at a time. But it didn't work. Bebe fell asleep.

Bebe started to dream. In her dream she was having a picnic in her room. She had prepared all her favorite kinds of chocolate. Suddenly a family of aliens crawled through the window. They were having a picnic, too. They sprinkled salt and pepper on Bebe. And then the biggest alien started to come toward her.

Bebe opened her eyes. She could see her armor.
She could see her bedroom door, open just right.
But when she looked down the hall, Bebe saw an
alien.
"I want Bebe for dinner," it cackled.
"MOTHER!" screamed Bebe.

Bebe's mother ran into the room and turned
on the light.

"Walter. Bed. Now!"

"I think you should lock him in the closet or
put him outside for the night," said Bebe.

"And I think *you* should go to sleep. Let's tuck
you in and give you one more kiss. Lights out,
and no more scary dreams."

Bebe knew that no one would
come to her rescue. Her mother didn't
understand. And all Walter cared about was
catching fish. The worms! Bebe had forgotten
to tell her mother about the garden! "I'll tell her
first thing tomorrow," thought Bebe.
But for now Bebe tried to think of ways to get rid of the aliens
AND Walter. She fell asleep before she ran out of ideas.

"Laser beams are in my eyes!" Bebe screamed.
She shot out of bed. But there were no laser beams,
only sunlight streaming in. It was morning.
Bebe looked around her room. She touched her arm and
wiggled her fingers. She had survived another night. But
she had to be careful. The aliens knew where she went
to school.

"Good morning," Bebe said to the bus driver. "Mind if I check under here?" She inspected under the bus before she climbed in.

When she got to school, she stayed far from the edge of the playground.

And she didn't put her hands in her cubby.

Bebe made it to recess without any alien sightings, but she knew they were there. Somewhere.

Her friends wanted her to play.

"Let's pretend all boys are diseases, and we have to find a cure," said Nora.

"Let's make perfume out of berry juice," said Alise.

"Let's see who can hold their breath the longest," said Edie.

"We are all in danger from aliens," said Bebe. "Let's go indoors and hide."

"Not again, Bebe," said Nora.
"You should do something about your alien problem," said Alise.
"They're just a bad dream," said Edie.
Bebe's friends ran off to have fun.

Bebe was all alone.
She knew they were right.
She had to do something. But what?

That night at dinner, Walter tormented Bebe as usual.
"I'm hungry, please pass the Bebe," he said in an alien-like
way.
Bebe ignored him. She wished the aliens would take him
to a distant galaxy on a one-way trip. She closed her eyes
and sent the aliens a mind message: "Take Walter, not me.
Take Walter, not me."

And then Bebe
got an idea.

Mom, Bebe's up to something

When Bebe got ready for bed, she put on
her pajamas. She did not put on her armor.
She did not put on her safety goggles.
"Good night, Mother. Good night, Walter,"
was all Bebe said.

It took forever for her mother
and Walter to go to bed. Bebe
was getting sleepy. "I have to
stay awake. I can't go to sleep,"
she thought. She quietly sang
songs—every song she knew,
ten times in a row.

When everyone fell asleep, Bebe got busy.

Bebe put on big, woolly socks over her slippers for extra
silence. She took out her art supplies. She made signs
with big arrows on big pieces of paper.

Very quietly, walking on tiptoe, Bebe moved all her toys
to Walter's room. Then she carefully covered Walter with
her blanket.
It was very late. Bebe went to bed, closed her eyes, and
fell asleep.

Bebe started to dream. In her dream she was sitting on a serving platter with lettuce leaves and cut radishes and cucumbers all around her. Aliens lined up with plates and forks. "Yummmmm," they said. "A delicious earthling Bebe."

"No, no, N-O, NO!" Bebe shouted, standing up. "You are in the wrong room. I am not Bebe. I am not delicious. I'll show you Bebe. She's very delicious!"

She led the aliens to Walter's room. "Here," she said,
pointing at Walter. "She's all yours. Have a nice snack."
She handed them doggie bags. "And if you ever come
back, **I'll eat YOU all for dinner!**"

The aliens trembled. They snatched Walter
and whooshed off in their UFO.
Bebe was safe at last.

When Bebe woke up the next morning,
she was as happy as could be.
"I smell waffles!" she said.

the aliens are far away,
Yay!
the aliens took Walter away
Yay!

Then, humming a tune,
Bebe marched downstairs
to breakfast.

"Mmmmmmmmmmm.
Bebe and waffles for
breakfast!" an alien-like
voice said.

Walter!
How could this be? Here was Walter sitting
at the table.
But Bebe had seen the aliens take him away.
Forever! She was sure. Bebe closed her eyes
and opened them again.
Walter was still there.

Maybe this was a dream. Maybe this, right here,
right now, was a dream. A terrible nightmare.
Could this be a terrible Walter-and-waffle
nightmare?

No, this was the real Walter.

Then . . . But . . . ? Bebe stared at Walter.
If this was really Walter, then the aliens . . .
Could the aliens have been . . . a dream?

The aliens must have been a dream.
The aliens were only a dream.
A bad dream.

"I was dreaming! I was dreaming! The aliens
are gone for good!" sang Bebe. "And I got
rid of them!"
She helped herself to the rest of the waffles.
Everything was perfect.

Well, almost everything. She still had Walter
to live with.

She spotted his can of worms by
the door.
And then Bebe got another idea.

Walter was in big trouble . . . and it was no dream.